The Frog Prince

STORY BY **THE BROTHERS GRIMM**
RETOLD BY **MARGRETE LAMOND**,
WITH **RUSSELL THOMSON**

PICTURES BY
DAVID CORNISH

LITTLE HARE
www.littleharebooks.com

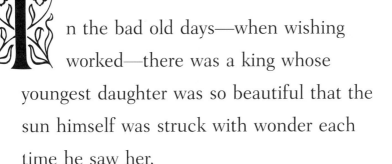 n the bad old days—when wishing worked—there was a king whose youngest daughter was so beautiful that the sun himself was struck with wonder each time he saw her.

Not far from the king's palace was a forest and there, under an ancient tree, was a deep, dark well. Whenever the day was hot, the princess would go to the well with her golden ball. She would throw the ball in the air and catch it, over and over again—it was her favourite thing to do.

One day, when she threw the ball up, it dropped to the ground, bounced, and then plunged into the deep, dark well.

The princess watched as it sank—deeper and deeper—until it vanished from sight completely.

The loss of her golden ball was such a shock that the princess let out a wail, and then another. Before long the wails had turned into a storm of grief that the princess couldn't find a way to stop.

Suddenly a voice cried out, 'What is the matter, princess? Your weeping is enough to melt a heart of stone.'

The princess looked around to see who was speaking, but all she could see was a frog sticking his ugly head out of the water in the well.

'I'm sad,' she said, 'because my golden
ball has fallen into the well and I can't
think how I will get it back.'

'I can easily fetch it,' said the frog. 'But
what will you give me in return?'

'Whatever you wish, dear frog,' she said.
'I'll give you my gown, my pearls and jewels,
even my crown.'

'They mean nothing to me,' said the frog.
'But if you promise to love me, and let me
be your companion, and let me sit beside
you and eat from your golden plate and
drink from your crystal cup; and if you will
let me creep into your soft white bed, then
I will fetch your ball from the well.'

'I'll promise you anything,' the princess said, but to herself she added, 'He is just a frog who sits in the water and croaks! He will never really do these things!'

So the frog dived to the bottom of the well and soon returned with the golden ball in his mouth.

The princess was so happy to see her ball again that she grabbed it and ran home.

'Wait!' cried the frog. 'You promised to take me with you!'

But the princess didn't hear a thing. She hurried home, and soon forgot the frog.

The next evening, the princess was at the table with the king and all the court.

She was eating from her golden plate and drinking from her crystal cup, when something was heard coming up the marble stairs.

Splitch-splotch, splitch-splotch, it went.

When it got to the top, it knocked on the door and cried, 'Open the door, youngest princess!'

The princess ran at once to see who was there. When she saw it was the frog, she slammed the door, ran back to her chair and bit her knuckles with fright.

'Dear child,' said the king, 'who has frightened you so? Was it an ogre come to take you away?'

'Nothing like that,' murmured the princess. 'Just an ugly old frog.'

'And why would a frog ask after you?' said the king.

'Yesterday, when I dropped my golden ball in the water,' said the princess, 'he fetched it for me, but only after I promised to let him be my companion. I never thought he meant it. And now he has climbed out of his well and wants to come in.'

Just then there was another knock at the door.

'Princess,' cried the frog. 'Have you forgotten the promise you made beside the well? Let me in!'

'What you have promised, you must uphold,' said the king. 'Go and let him in.'

The princess went and opened the door and in hopped the frog.

'Lift me to your lap,' he croaked.

The princess could hardly bear to look at him, let alone pick him up. But the king told her to do as she was asked.

Then the frog said, 'Now slide your golden plate closer, that I might share your meal.'

She did as she was bid, but everyone could see she was unwilling.

They saw, too, how much the frog enjoyed his meal, but how every morsel stuck fast in the princess' throat.

At last the frog said, 'I've eaten my fill, and now I'm tired. Take me to your chamber, so that I might creep with you between the clean white sheets.'

The princess began to wail, and wail some more. She was terrified of the ugly frog, and couldn't bear to touch him, let alone sleep beside him in her bed.

But her father had no patience. 'What you have promised, you must uphold,' he said.

Whether she wanted to or not, the princess had to lead the frog to her chamber. But once she was out of sight of her father, she picked up the frog between two fingers and placed him in a dusty corner.

Then she crept alone between the sheets.

No sooner had she done so than she heard *splitch-splotch, splitch-splotch* as the frog hopped across the floor.

'Have you forgotten the promise you made?' he croaked. 'If you don't do as you promised, I will tell your father.'

At that, the princess lost her temper. She snatched up the frog and hurled him against the wall with all her might. 'Will you be quiet, you ghastly frog!' she shrieked.

But what smacked against the wall was no longer a frog. It was a fine-looking prince, healthy and tall, whose eyes shone with gratitude.

'I was cursed,' he said, 'to remain a frog, until a princess lost her temper with me. Will you now promise to love me, and let me be your companion, and let me eat from your golden plate and drink from your crystal cup and sleep in your soft white bed?'

The princess promised with all of her heart. So, in the morning, along came a carriage to fetch the prince and the princess home to his kingdom. It was drawn by eight white horses, and at the back stood Iron Henry, the prince's loyal servant.

Off they went, but they hadn't gone far before there was a loud bang.

'Is the axel broken?' cried the prince.

'No, master,' said Iron Henry. 'It was just one of the bands I bound around my chest.'

You see, so loyal was Iron Henry that, long ago, when his master was turned into a frog, he placed three iron bands around his chest to prevent his heart from breaking with grief.

Twice more there was a loud bang and, each time, the prince thought the carriage was breaking. But it was only the bands around Iron Henry's chest that had burst, because he was so relieved that his prince was free and happy at last.

Little Hare Books
an imprint of
Hardie Grant Egmont
Ground Floor, Building 1, 658 Church Street
Richmond, Victoria 3121, Australia

www.littleharebooks.com

Cataloguing-in-Publication details are available from the
National Library of Australia

978-1-742974-02-6 (hbk.)

Designed by Vida & Luke Kelly
Produced by Pica Digital, Singapore
Printed in China by Wai Man Book Binding Ltd.

5 4 3 2 1